Mountain Mona

Written by Vivian French

Illustrated by Chris Fisher

Collins

Chapter 1

Mona was a goat. She lived at the top of a mountain
with her brother, her sister and her mother.
Her brother was good at jumping.
Her sister was good at leaping.
Her mother was good at climbing and scrambling.

Mona didn't think she was good at ANYTHING ...
except growing flowers.
Mona grew big yellow sunflowers – huge yellow
sunflowers that nodded in the sunshine.
Mona loved them. She fed them and watered them.
She watched them grow ... and she smiled.

"Mona," said her brother, "goats don't grow flowers.
JUMPING is what goats do. If a fierce lion comes
along, goats must JUMP out of the way. Jumping is
easy peasy. Watch me jump over this bush!"
Mona looked round.

"What bush?" she asked.

"THIS bush," replied her brother.

"Oh," said Mona. "I thought it was a rock."

Mona's brother jumped over the bush.

"There!" he said. "Now you try!"

Mona tried …

"OW!" she said.

"You should look where you're jumping," said her brother.

"I did!" Mona replied, and she went to see her sunflowers.

Chapter 2

"Mona," said her sister, "goats don't grow flowers.
LEAPING is what goats do. If a fierce lion comes
along, goats must LEAP out of the way. Leaping is
easy peasy. Watch me leap from rock to rock!"
Mona looked round.
"What rocks?" she asked.
"THESE rocks," said her sister.
"Oh," said Mona. "I thought they were bushes."

Mona's sister leapt from rock to rock.
"There!" she said. "Now you try."
Mona tried ...

"OW!" she said.
"You should look where you're leaping,"
said her sister.
"I DID!" replied Mona, and she went to see her
sunflowers.

8

"Mona," said her mother, "why don't you try climbing and scrambling?"
Mona sighed a huge sigh.
"All right," she said. "I'll try."

Mona began to climb, but she fell on a thistle.

She tried to scramble, but she bumped her nose.

"It's no good," she said. "I can't do the things other
goats can. Besides, I don't LIKE jumping …
or leaping … or climbing … or scrambling.
And I don't care about fierce lions either.
AND I don't like living on the top of a mountain.
Mountains make me dizzy."
Mona stomped off down the mountain.

Chapter 3

At the bottom of the mountain was a lion.

A great big fierce lion.

A great big fierce lion wearing spectacles.

A great big fierce lion wearing spectacles, who opened his mouth WIDE and showed his SHARP teeth.

Mona didn't move. She stood quite still and smiled.
"Excuse me," said the lion, "but please don't smile.
PLEASE run away. And please do it NOW!"
"Why?" said Mona.
"Because," said the lion, "that's what goats do.
They run away. Then big fierce lions chase them."

Mona frowned. "Are you a lion?"

"YES," said the lion. "What did you think I was?"

"Well," said Mona, "I thought you were
a sunflower."

"A SUNFLOWER?" The lion looked angry.

"I'm a BIG FIERCE LION!"

Mona looked at the lion more closely.

"I thought you were a BIG sunflower," she said.

The lion sat down. "This is terrible," he said. "How can I scare anyone if I look like a sunflower?" Mona thought hard.

"Maybe I'm no good at being scared," she said, quietly. "After all, I'm no good at jumping or leaping or climbing or scrambling. Maybe I'm no good at being scared either."

"Hmm," growled the lion. "But ..." He began to look excited. "What if it's something else? What if you're no good at SEEING things?"

"What do you mean?" asked Mona.

"You thought I was a sunflower, didn't you? Here, try on my spectacles!"

"All right," said Mona.

She put on the spectacles.

Chapter 4

"WOW!" Mona said.
"WOW! I can see for MILES!"
She looked all around.
"WOW! WOW! WOW!"
"Stop saying WOW," said the lion,
"and look at me."
Mona looked at the lion.
"WOW," she said, and she sprang
in the air. "You ARE a big
fierce lion."

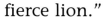

And Mona jumped ...

... and leapt

... and climbed

... and scrambled all the way to the very top of the mountain.

"OI!" roared the lion.
"Bring back my spectacles!"
Mona stood on one leg on
the very highest rock.
"You look MUCH fiercer without them!"
she shouted, loudly.
"Oh," purred the lion. "Do I?"
And he slipped
... and he staggered
... and he fell over thistles and bushes,
all the way back down to his cave.

19

Mona stood on her rock and shouted to her brother, her sister and her mother.

"Look at me!" she said. "I can jump! And I can leap! And climb! And scramble! I can do all the things goats are meant to do!"

"WOW!" said her brother and sister.

"Good," said her mother. "But there's something else you're VERY good at."

"Is there?" asked Mona. "What's that?"

"Getting rid of big fierce lions!" said her mother, with a huge smile.

Mountain Mona

The Leaping Rocks

The Scrambling Rocks

Mona's Sunflowers

Mona's Rock

The Lion's Cave

The Jumping Bushes

23

Getting creative

- If your child's enjoyed reading about Mona and the lion, they could try making up another adventure for her.

- They could start by planning what might happen in another story, when Mona meets a mountain bear. How might she scare him away?

- They could draw a story map for the new adventure. This will help children to plan the story and use their imagination.

- Once they've got a plan, encourage them to start writing the story, including pictures if they like.

Other books at Level 3:

Fiction	Non-fiction
Twinkle, Twinkle Firefly — Poems by John Agard and Grace Nichols, Illustrated by Satoshi Kitamura	What's that Building? — Richard Platt, Future Studio
Chewy Hughie — Jane Clarke, Sarah McConnell	Unusual Traditions
Mountain Mona — Vivian French, Chris Fisher	How to be a Knight in 10 easy stages — Scoular Anderson